Li
the Labrador
Fairy

By Daisy Meadows

ORCHARD

www.orchardseriesbooks.co.uk

Jack Frost's Ode

Puppy care sounds dull and dreary.
Training rules just make me weary.
These fairies must be made to see
No puppy matters more than me!

The fairies dared to tell me "no",
So far away their pups will go.
And if they don't do what I say,
I'll yell at them till they obey!

Contents

Chapter One
Leafy Lane

It was a fresh spring day in Tippington, and Rachel Walker was walking along Leafy Lane with her best friend, Kirsty Tate. The sun was shining, a little breeze ruffled the leaves, and the trees were thick with pink blossom.

"I'm so glad you're staying with me

for the whole of half term," said Rachel, smiling at Kirsty.

"Me too," said Kirsty. "We always have the most exciting adventures together."

The girls had been friends ever since they had first met the Rainbow Fairies and become friends of Fairyland. But today's adventure was nothing to do with fairy magic. They were on their way to the Leafy Lane Animal Shelter, where they had volunteered to help for a few days.

"Looking after tiny puppies is going to be one of our loveliest adventures ever," Rachel added.

A litter of newborn puppies had been rescued, and Rachel had read about it in the local newspaper. The shelter manager had asked for volunteers to care for them until they found new homes, so Rachel and Kirsty had offered their help for the week of half term.

"There it is," said Kirsty as they rounded a bend in the lane.

The Leafy Lane Animal Shelter was a long, low building with a green roof and red brick walls. The door was open, and a young man was standing in the doorway. He had blonde hair and he was wearing a T-shirt and a pair of cargo shorts.

"Hi, I'm Nate," he said, shaking their hands. "You're Rachel and Kirsty, right? Thanks for being here. I'm super busy trying to look after all the animals."

"Just tell us what you want us to do," said Rachel, smiling.

"I'd like you to feed the puppies and keep them warm and clean," said Nate. "Apart from that, for now they just need quiet time and a bit of handling. They're very young."

He led them to a reception desk and picked up a tray of bottles filled with milk. Then Rachel and Kirsty followed him to a clean kennel room with a glass door. Inside, there was a wooden nesting box. The girls peered over and saw five white puppies with pink noses, snuggling together on a cosy blanket.

"They're adorable," said Kirsty in a whisper. "What breed are they?"

"They're mixed breed," said Nate. "It means that their parents were probably different breeds."

"Will they stay the same colour?" asked Rachel.

"They might," said Nate, kneeling down beside the puppies. "But I've known puppies to change colour as they get older. That's part of the fun of seeing a

puppy grow."

"They're so tiny," said Kirsty, getting down on her hands and knees.

Nate very gently picked one of them up. She wriggled and squeaked.

"They need milk every two hours," he said. "It's time for their feed now. These bottles are full of puppy milk substitute."

Nate picked up the first bottle.

"Hold the puppy on your lap and keep the bottle upright, like this," he said. "Don't squeeze the bottle. Just let the puppy suck it out slowly."

The puppy lay on her tummy, sucking

the milk happily.

"She's making such sweet little noises," said Rachel.

"Can we try?" asked Kirsty.

"Sure," said Nate. "Pick a puppy and a bottle."

The girls' hearts were fluttering with excitement, but they knew that staying calm was best for the puppies. They copied what Nate was doing, and soon had all three puppies enjoying their milk.

"I think this might be the most gorgeous thing I've ever done," Kirsty whispered.

When Nate's puppy stopped feeding, he burped her and helped her to go to the toilet.

"You've both got the hang of it," he said with a smile. "I'm going to leave you to get on with it, but I won't be far away."

Rachel and Kirsty burped their puppies and helped them to go to the toilet, just as Nate had shown them. Then they picked up the last two puppies and started to feed them. Other dogs were barking in the distance, but the little white-brick kennel room was a safe, quiet space.

"I wonder who their new families will

be," said Kirsty. "They will need lots of things."

"A bed, a harness, a collar, a food bowl . . ." Rachel began.

"And a water bowl," Kirsty added. "Food, toys, treats — it must be fun picking them all out."

"I wish we could have one," said Rachel. "But Buttons is enough to keep us busy!"

Buttons was Rachel's shaggy, mischievous dog.

Kirsty smiled.

"I don't think that Pearl would like it if I brought a puppy home," she said.

Pearl, Kirsty's black-and-white cat, had been with her since the girls' adventure with Pearl the Cloud Fairy.

When the puppies had snuggled up for

another snooze, the girls picked up the
empty bottles and turned to leave. As
they passed a pile of fresh blankets, one
of them moved.

"Is that another puppy?" asked Kirsty.

She lifted the corner of the blanket and
a bright glow filled the room as a little
fairy fluttered out. She glanced at the
nest box with sparkling brown eyes.

"Hi," she said softly. "I'm Li the
Labrador Fairy."

Chapter Two
The Puppy Care Fair

Li had long dark-brown hair and delicate pale-green wings. She was wearing a stripy blue and white shirt, blue jeans with a tan belt, and white trainers. A sleek golden Labrador puppy was tucked under her arm.

"It's nice to meet you," Rachel said.

"You too," said Li. "I've heard lots about you in Fairyland."

Her puppy gave a little woof.

"He wants to be introduced too," said Li with a laugh. "This is Buddy."

Rachel stroked him with a fingertip, and he licked her with his tiny pink tongue.

"Hello, Buddy," said Kirsty. "You're beautiful."

"Thanks," said Li. "I'm one of the Puppy Care Fairies, and we help owners in the fairy and human worlds to look after their puppies and teach them about exercise, grooming, training and health.

It's my job to help with exercise."

"Are you here to check up on these puppies?" Rachel asked, glancing at the snoozing litter.

"No, I know they're in safe hands," said Li. "I've come to invite you to the Puppy Care Fair. We've set up stalls to help visitors learn how to look after puppies."

"That would be perfect," said Kirsty. "We want to find out as much as we can about helping the Leafy Lane pups."

"And no time will pass in the human world while we're in Fairyland," Rachel remembered. "We'll come back to this exact moment."

Li clapped her hands together happily. Then she nodded at Buddy, who let out a quiet yap. The silver tennis-ball tag on his green collar glowed softly.

"Oh," said Kirsty in a surprised voice.

A magical ribbon of sparkling fairy dust rippled from Buddy's tag and coiled around the girls. They felt their delicate wings unfurling, and their bodies shrank to fairy size.

"Buddy's collar carries the magic that helps me to do my job," Li explained. "He has a little magic of his own when he's wearing it."

"What sort of magic can Buddy do?" Kirsty asked.

"Put your hands on his collar," said Li, smiling.

Rachel and Kirsty touched the green collar and were instantly spun around so fast that everything became a blur. When they stopped, the white-brick kennel room had vanished. They were standing in a daisy-filled meadow, surrounded by candy-striped stalls. Crowds of fairies and goblins were mingling around the stalls, and dogs and puppies were running, sniffing and playing in all directions.

"Welcome back to Fairyland," said Li.

Rachel and Kirsty hardly knew which way to look. There were so many wonderful things to see. The smaller stalls were filled with collars, leads, bowls, coats and beds, as well as balls, chew toys and soft blankets. The bigger stalls were numbered, and Li led Rachel and Kirsty to stall one.

"This is my stall," she said. "Each of the Puppy Care Fairies is doing training lessons today. When a visitor has done the training, they get a stamp. If they collect all four stamps, they get a certificate that says they are ready to adopt a puppy."

"That's a great way to make sure that everyone is ready for a new puppy," said Rachel. "What are you teaching them?"

"How much exercise puppies need,"
said Li. "Buddy's glad to help of course –
he's full of beans!"

She laughed and ruffled Buddy's golden
coat.

A small crowd had already gathered, so
Li stepped behind her stall.

"Welcome, everyone," she said. "I'm
going to tell you how to keep your

puppy fit and healthy."

Rachel and Kirsty listened as Li
explained how to exercise puppies. Then
she asked the visitors questions to check
that they had understood.

"Why is exercise so important?" she
asked.

A goblin standing next to Rachel and
Kirsty put up his hand.

"Because it keeps puppies healthy," he
shouted out.

"Right," said Li, smiling. "And can you
tell me how long a puppy walk should
be?"

The goblin's hand shot up again.

"Five minutes for every month of age,"
he squawked.

"That's right," said Li. "Here's a free gift
for being such a great listener."

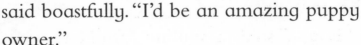

She handed him
a green T-shirt
that said "I Love
Puppies" on the
front.

"You did really
well," said Kirsty.

The goblin
whirled around.

"Yes, I know," he
said boastfully. "I'd be an amazing puppy
owner."

"We're looking after some puppies in
the Leafy Lane Animal Shelter," said
Rachel. "They're really sweet."

Kirsty was thinking about all the
goblins at the fair.

"Is Jack Frost here?" she asked.

"Yes," said the goblin. "He really wants

a puppy too."

The goblin slipped away as Li joined them.

"I need to stay at my stall," she said. "But you should look around and visit the other Puppy Fairy stalls. Have fun!"

Chapter Three
Jack Frost is Angry

First, the girls visited the magical dog toys stall. There were chewable bones that changed colour with every chew, cuddly toys that turned into a different animal whenever the puppy barked, and self-throwing balls that bounced away from the catcher.

"Buttons would love these," said Rachel.

They stopped at stall two and watched Frenchie the Bulldog Fairy making healthy dog treats with Pepper, her French bulldog.

"Look, Frenchie's collar is red," Rachel noticed. "And her silver tag is in the shape of a bone."

"Each magical puppy must have a different tag," said Kirsty. "Let's see what the others are."

At stall three, Seren the Sausage Dog Fairy was grooming her puppy, Wiggles. His collar was yellow with a silver comb dog tag. Pandora the Poodle Fairy was at stall four, showing how to train a puppy to walk calmly on a lead. Her puppy, Cleo, had a blue collar with a silver whistle tag.

"I want to meet them all," said Kirsty.

"Me too," said Rachel. "But their stalls are really crowded. Let's get something to

eat and then come back."

There were freshly baked mini pasties, jam tarts, dog-paw-shaped sandwiches and even bowls of bogmallows for the goblins. Rachel chose a sausage roll and Kirsty picked some falafels. They walked around the stalls again, enjoying hearing the happy woofs of dogs and the friendly chatter around them. Then they walked back towards Li's stall.

"Who's that talking to Li?" Kirsty asked.

A tall figure in a long cloak was facing Li, waving his arms around.

"Stop telling me what to do," he shouted. "My puppy will have to walk itself. I'm too busy and important to do that."

"It's not safe," Li said in a calm voice.

"I can't give you a stamp until you understand what a puppy needs."

"It's Jack Frost," said Rachel, with a sudden shiver.

Grey mist started to swirl around Jack Frost's feet, and the grass beneath him turned from green to frosty white.

"I don't care about stamps," he yelled. "I just want a puppy."

"You have to collect the stamps to get a certificate," said Li. "It wouldn't be fair on the puppy to take it without knowing how to look after it."

Jack Frost snarled and spun around

on his heel. Then he snapped his fingers,
which flashed with blue lightning.
Goblins came running from all directions.
They scampered around Jack Frost as
he strode off. Kirsty and Rachel hurried
over to Li.

"He's up to something," said Rachel.

Li linked arms with them and looked
around at the busy fair.

"I'm sure there's nothing to worry
about," she said, smiling. "After all, what
can he do in front of all these fairies?"

Half an hour later, it looked as if Li
had been right. Jack Frost had completely
disappeared.

"He's probably gone back to the Ice
Castle in a huff," said Rachel. "Oh look,
there are the Dance Fairies."

They fluttered over to say hello. Zainab

the Squishy Toy Fairy joined them, and soon lots of their fairy friends had gathered around. Rachel and Kirsty were enjoying some iced raspberry pop and pink macaroons with the Sweet Fairies when they heard Li's voice ringing out across the meadow.

"Buddy? Buddy! Where are you?"

Rachel and Kirsty zoomed to her side. She was standing beside her stall, looking perplexed.

"What's wrong?" asked Rachel.

"I don't know where he's gone," she said. "I was talking to a goblin about how to make exercise fun for a puppy, and I wasn't watching Buddy. When I turned around, he was gone."

"Do you think he's lost?" Kirsty asked.

"No, he's probably run off to try to

find a pair of shoes," said Li. "Buddy is obsessed with shoes."

"We'll help you to find him," said Rachel.

The three fairies flew around the fair, checking all the places where a mischievous puppy might hide. But there was no sign of Buddy.

"Pepper!" called a voice behind them.

Li, Rachel and Kirsty spun around and saw Frenchie fluttering behind them.

"Have you seen my puppy?' she asked when she saw them. "I was answering a goblin's questions about how to help a poorly puppy, and when he left, Frenchie had vanished."

"Maybe Buddy and Pepper are off causing puppy mischief together somewhere," said Li.

A third voice rang out across the meadow.

"Wiggles!" Seren was calling. "Wiggles, come here please!"

The fairies fluttered over to Seren, who was weaving through the crowd.

"A goblin asked me how to groom every sort of dog," she said. "I had just reached 'chow chows' when I realised that Wiggles wasn't in his basket."

The fairies exchanged a worried glance.

"This can't be a coincidence," said Kirsty. "We have to get to Pandora before the same thing happens to Cleo."

Chapter Four
Jack Frost's Revenge

They all flew towards the fourth stall.

"I see Pandora," Rachel exclaimed.
"She's talking to a goblin."

"Pandora!" cried Li.

The goblin glanced over his shoulder
at them and then slipped behind the stall.
Pandora smiled and waved to them as

they landed beside her.

"What's wrong?" she asked when she saw their worried faces.

"Is Cleo OK?" asked Li.

"Yes," said Pandora, looking surprised. "She just went to get a drink of water."

"I've got a bad feeling about this," said Kirsty. "Come on."

She and Rachel hurried around to the back of the stall, and the other fairies followed them. A silver water bowl was lying upside down on the grass.

"Where's Cleo?" asked Pandora in a shaky voice. "She should be here."

"Each of you was distracted by a goblin," said Rachel. "I don't think that's a coincidence."

"Clever little fairy," hissed a cruel voice. They whirled around to see Jack Frost

cackling with laughter. An icy, grey fog swirled around him.

"You'll be sorry for trying to stop me," he said, jabbing his bony finger at Li. "Now I have four puppies."

"Give them back!" exclaimed Li, bravely stepping forwards.

"Too late," Jack Frost gloated. "My goblins have orders to hide them away and train them for me. When they are obedient, they will live in my castle and I will use their magic for myself."

"No!" cried Rachel and Kirsty together.

"Yes!" Jack Frost retorted.

He gave another cruel, cackling laugh, and then vanished in a flash of blue lightning. The fairies stared at each other in horror.

"The poor puppies," said Kirsty, putting her hands to her mouth. "They'll be so frightened."

"Without their magical collars, we can't help them," said Li. "We can't look after any puppies anywhere."

"What can we do?" Pandora asked.

"We have no idea where the goblins have hidden them," Frenchie said with a groan. "It's hopeless."

She sank down on to a hay bale and buried her head in her hands.

"There's always hope," said Rachel in a determined voice. "Kirsty and I have

helped stop Jack
Frost before, and I
know we can do it
again."

"We'll find the
puppies and the
magical collars,"
said Kirsty.

Li threw her arms
around them in a
fierce hug.

"Thank you so much," she said. "We've
never had anything to do with Jack Frost
before."

"I know he can be scary," said Rachel.
"But when you stand up to him you find
out he's just a big bully."

"I can be brave for the puppies," said Li.
"But how are we going to find them?"

"We don't know whether he's hidden them here or in the human world," said Kirsty. "Let's split into two groups. How about we go back to the human world with Li, and Frenchie, Seren and Pandora stay here to search Fairyland?"

The fairies exchanged looks and then everyone nodded.

"We'll go and tell the visitors that the fair is over," said Frenchie. "Good luck in the human world."

Li raised her wand like a pen and drew a silvery puppy in the air. It romped away from them, leaving a sparkling trail of pawprints.

"Follow the puppy," called Li.

Chapter Five
Puppies in Danger

Moments later, the dazzling pawprints had led them back to the white-brick kennel room at the Leafy Lane Animal Shelter. The girls were human sized again, and Li was fluttering beside them.

"The puppies are still asleep," said Rachel in a whisper.

The nesting box was quiet and peaceful. Each fluffy little pup looked well-fed and happy. Li put her hand over her heart.

"They remind me of Buddy when he's asleep," she said, and her voice shook.

"I know we'll find him safe and sound," said Kirsty. "But first, we should check if Nate has a job for us. We said that we would help out and we mustn't break our promise."

"I'm going to be brave for Buddy," said Li, wiping tears from her eyes. "I'll keep out of sight."

She slipped into Rachel's backpack. The girls left the kennel room and shut the door carefully behind them. Then they walked through the building, looking for Nate.

"We might have to search for a while,"

said Kirsty. "He's super busy because there aren't enough staff."

But when they reached the reception desk, they stopped in surprise. Nate was leaning back on a chair with his feet up on the desk. His eyes were closed and he was gently snoring, a newspaper strewn on the floor.

"I thought he was busy," Kirsty whispered.

Rachel cleared her throat, and Nate's eyes flickered open.

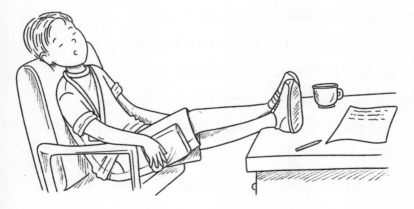

"Everything all right, girls?" he asked, yawning and stretching.

"The puppies are asleep," said Rachel. "Nate, could you spare us for a little while? We need to help a friend with something."

"No problem," said Nate, waving his hand airily. "The puppies can look after themselves."

"Really?" asked Kirsty. "I thought they needed someone to watch over them."

"They'll be fine," said Nate carelessly. "Besides, another volunteer has just arrived. Funny boy – he's dressed in green from head to foot."

"Where is he?" asked Rachel. "We should tell him what time the puppies last had their milk."

"He wanted to look at the exercise

48

area," said Nate, jerking his thumb towards a side door.

He picked up his newspaper and started to read. Feeling confused, the girls went through the door and found themselves in a long garden, surrounded by a high fence.

"What's the matter with Nate?" asked Kirsty as soon as the door shut behind them. "He seems more interested in his newspaper than the puppies."

"It's because the magical collars are missing," said Li, peeping out of the backpack. "Without them, humans will forget how to care for puppies."

"Look," said Rachel.

She pointed to the far end of the garden, where a boy was playing with a Labrador puppy. The boy was wearing a green cap, green shorts and a green T-shirt that said "I Love Puppies" on the front.

"That's not a boy," said Kirsty. "It's a goblin."

"Oh my goodness," Li exclaimed. "He's with Buddy!"

"It's the goblin we met at your stall, Li," said Kirsty. "He must have remembered what we said about the animal shelter."

"Let's go and find out what he's doing

here," said Rachel.
They walked
up behind the
goblin. Buddy's
green collar and
tennis-ball-shaped
tag were shining
in the sunlight. As
they got closer,
they heard the

goblin speaking to the puppy.

"You're going to be the best trained out
of all the puppies," he was saying. "I'll
make the people who work here show
me how to do it. Jack Frost won't let me
have a puppy of my own, but you're the
next best thing."

"He's not yours," said Kirsty.

The goblin spun around with a squawk

of fright. When he saw the girls, his eyes narrowed and he folded his arms.

"Oh, it's you nosy parkers," he snapped. "Go away."

"You don't understand," said Rachel. "You say you love puppies, but you're putting them in danger. While you have Buddy, people all over the world are forgetting how to care for their puppies."

"Who cares as long as I've got a puppy?" said the goblin. "Now leave us alone. It's time for our walk."

He clipped a lead on to the green collar and

pulled Buddy out of a gate at the side of the garden. He left the gate swinging wide open.

"We have to follow him," said Kirsty. "But what about the puppies here?"

"There's time before they need another feed," said Li.

The girls ran to catch up with the goblin, being careful to close the gate behind them.

"He's walking in to town," said Rachel.

They followed the goblin down Leafy Lane, on to the pavement and towards the shops. After ten minutes, Buddy was tired. He dragged on the lead, and then sat down. The goblin pulled something out of his pocket.

"He's remembering what Pandora said about using treats to help with training,"

said Kirsty.

"But he's forgotten what Frenchie said about chocolate," said Rachel. "Stop!"

She ran forward and knocked the chocolate out of the goblin's hand.

"Chocolate is poisonous for dogs," she said. "It can make them really poorly."

"I know that," squawked the goblin untruthfully. "I've got other treats."

He stomped off, pulling Buddy along after him. Li looked out of Rachel's backpack and groaned.

"Oh no, is that a shoe shop up ahead?" she asked with a groan. "Buddy loves shoes."

"Ahh, that's sweet," said Kirsty.

"No, you don't understand," said Li. "Buddy really, really loves shoes, and I haven't trained him out of it."

Buddy suddenly darted sideways in to the shop. The goblin was yanked off his feet.

"The goblin has to get him out of there or he'll chew everything he sees," cried Li.

Chapter Six
Shoe Crazy!

The shoe shop was in pandemonium.
Buddy was going mad with the pure joy
of having so many shoes to play with.

He bit them, he chewed them, he shook
them and he threw them. He grabbed
a mouthful of slippers and ran in circles
around the shop, tripping up the shoppers

as he dropped them in his wake.

The shop assistants and the goblin chased him as the shoppers fell over. Buddy was having the time of his life and every toddler in the shop was crying with laughter. The goblin stopped chasing the puppy and started giggling too.

Rachel ran into the shop.

"You have to stop him!" she exclaimed

to the goblin. "It's not funny."

"Leave me alone," the goblin shouted.
"Stop telling me what to do. You're not
the boss of me!"

"No, but Jack Frost is," said Rachel.
"And he is going to be cross with you if
you don't train the puppy."

The goblin stopped laughing.

"Hey, puppy, come here," he squawked.

Buddy didn't even hear him. The
goblin's shoulders sagged.

"He's not listening," he said. "Jack Frost
will explode if I don't train this puppy."

"Give me the treats," said Rachel.
"Maybe I can get him to come to me."

"No way," the goblin snapped. "They're
mine."

"I don't think Buddy will listen to me
without treats," said Rachel. "He would

listen to Li, but she can't appear in front of all these people."

Suddenly, Rachel heard Li's calm voice in her ear.

"Quickly, lift me on to the goblin's shoulder," she said. "I've got an idea."

Rachel cupped her hands and the tiny fairy fluttered into them. Checking to make sure that no one was watching, she lifted Li on to the goblin's shoulder. Li tucked herself behind his large, pointed ear.

"Listen to her," said Rachel.

She slipped back outside and watched as the goblin stepped forwards, holding a dog treat in his hand.

"Buddy," he called in a loud, firm voice. "Buddy, heel."

Buddy stopped and looked at the goblin.

"Good boy," said the goblin again.

He showed Buddy the treat he was holding.

"Li's whispering in his ear," Rachel told Kirsty. "She's telling him what to do."

They watched the little puppy bound over to the goblin and sit beside him. The goblin picked up his lead and then gave him the treat. Then they walked out of the shop and stopped in front of the girls. The goblin was sweating.

"I did it," he said, panting. "I made him come to me."

Kirsty pulled the goblin out of sight around the corner, and Li peeped out from behind his ear.

"Woof!" said Buddy when he saw her. "Woof! Woof!"

His tail wagged so fast that it was a blur, and he gazed up at her adoringly. The goblin stared at him. Then he held out the lead to Rachel. She took it in astonishment.

"I . . . er . . . think maybe there's more to learn about training a puppy than I thought," he muttered. "It's not just about putting a lead on. I'm not ready to be a puppy owner. I need to learn how to look after one first."

Li leaned forwards and gave the goblin a tiny butterfly kiss.

"You've done the right thing for Buddy," she said. "To say thank you, I will give you puppy-care lessons myself, until you are ready to look after a puppy of your own."

The goblin smiled, and his cheeks turned from green to rosy pink.

"I saw a pet shop further up the road," he exclaimed. "I'm going to choose a collar for my future puppy!"

He sprinted off, and Li fluttered down to Buddy.

"I'm so happy that we found you," she said, burying her head in his silky fur.

As soon as she touched him, he shrank to fairy size. She gathered him into her

arms and he licked her face, going mad with happy woofs. Li was half-laughing and half-crying with joy.

"I was broken-hearted without him," she said to the girls. "You've made everything right again. Thank you a million times over."

"We're so glad we could help," said Kirsty.

"I've put everything back to normal in the shoe shop," said Li with a bright smile. "Now I can take Buddy home."

She waved her wand and disappeared

back to Fairyland. Rachel and Kirsty looked at each other and then shared a delighted hug.

"Thank goodness we found Buddy," said Kirsty. "I hope that we can find the other three puppies quickly."

"Me too," said Rachel. "But for now, we ought to get back to the shelter. I just hope another Puppy Care Fairy turns up soon."

"They will," said Kirsty. "I'm sure that our next puppy adventure is just around the corner!"

The End

**Now it's time for Kirsty and
Rachel to help...**

Frenchie the Bulldog Fairy

Read on for a sneak peek...

"I wish it would stop pouring," said
Rachel Walker. "It would be much nicer
for the animals if it was sunny."

Rain was drumming on the roof of the
Leafy Lane Animal Shelter, where Rachel
and her best friend Kirsty Tate were
volunteering over half term. They had
offered to help care for some newborn
puppies who didn't have a mother. This
morning, they were busy cleaning the
kennel while the puppies snoozed. The
shelter manager, Nate, was playing with
the older dogs in the rain.

"They don't mind a few drops of water," said Kirsty, looking out of the kennel window. "They're having fun."

"I'm glad we volunteered," said Rachel, sweeping the floor. "The puppies are gorgeous, and we wouldn't have met the Puppy Care Fairies if we hadn't come."

The day before, Li the Labrador Fairy had invited them to the Puppy Care Fair in Fairyland. While they were there, Jack Frost had stolen the fairies' puppies and their magical collars. He was angry that they wouldn't let him adopt a puppy without learning how to take care of it. Four of Jack Frost's goblins had taken the puppies and were training them for Jack Frost.

"I'm glad we managed to help Li," said Kirsty. "It's lovely to think that Buddy and his magical collar are back where they belong."

"But there are still three missing puppies and collars," said Rachel. "Until we find them, the fairies won't be able to look after puppies around the world."

"We're going to find them," said Kirsty, covering the puppies with fresh blankets. "We won't let the fairies down."

The girls left the puppies fast asleep and took the dirty blankets and towels to the laundry room. Most of the washing machines were already full.

"Here's an empty one," said Rachel.

But before they could put the blankets and towels in, the machine started to spin by itself. The girls dropped their laundry and knelt down in front of it.

"Could it have been set to turn itself on

at a certain time?" asked Kirsty.

"But there's nothing inside," said Rachel. "Or is there . . .?"

Slowly, a blur of sparkling rainbow colours appeared inside the machine. Then the machine door burst open. The colours kept spinning as the sparkles spelled out two words:

PLEASE HELP!

"One of the fairies needs us," said Rachel at once.

"Fairyland, here we come," said Kirsty.

They opened the lockets that Queen Titania had given them. They were filled with just enough fairy dust to carry the girls to Fairyland. Without hesitating, Rachel and Kirsty sprinkled fairy dust over themselves. It gave them a warm, tickly feeling as they shrank to fairy size, with shimmering wings that lifted them into the air.

"Oh, something's pulling me," Rachel exclaimed.

"Me too," said Kirsty. "I think it's the rainbow whirl."

The shimmering colours were still spinning inside the machine, and now they were being pulled inside.

Read Frenchie the Bulldog Fairy to find out what adventures are in store for Kirsty and Rachel!

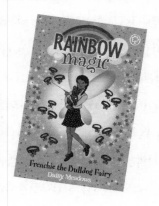

**Now it's time for Kirsty and
Rachel to help...**

Seren the Sausage Dog Fairy

Read on for a sneak peek...

"I think this might actually be the best
shop in the world," said Kirsty Tate.

She turned slowly on the spot, smiling
at shelves lined with pet toys, collars and
leads; tanks teeming with jewel-bright
fish; and pens filled with fluffy rabbits
and guinea pigs. Her best friend, Rachel
Walker, ran her hand over a pile of soft
puppy bedding.

"Buttons loves it in here," she said.
"Most shops don't let dogs in, but here
they always make a fuss of him."

Kirsty darted over to a display of tiny

velvet cat collars.

"These would look so cute on Pearl,"
she said, running her fingers along the
row.

Rachel crouched down to look at some
dog treats. Then she shook her head and
stood up again.

"I could spend hours in here," she said.
"But we have to get on with our errand.
Nate is relying on us."

Nate was the manager of the Leafy
Lane Animal Shelter, where Rachel and
Kirsty were volunteering for a few days.
The shelter had rescued a litter of tiny
newborn puppies, and Nate needed
lots of help. He had given them a list of
things to buy from the pet shop. Kirsty
took it out of her pocket and read aloud.

"Five puppy collars," she said. "One

pack of puppy pads, one puppy comb, one pack of puppy milk formula—"

"Not so fast!" said Rachel, who was pushing the shopping trolley. "I'm still looking at the collars."

Kirsty giggled and came over to help pick five colourful collars for the white puppies at the shelter.

"Red, yellow, pink, green and blue," she said as she dropped them in to the trolley. "They'll look like a little rainbow."

Soon the trolley was filled with puppy supplies.

"And last of all, a jumbo pack of sanitising wipes," said Rachel, adding them to the pile. "Wow, our arms will be aching after carrying all this back to the shelter."

Just then, they heard a great

commotion. People were shouting, and
dogs were barking and whining.

"What on earth is going on?" Kirsty
asked.

They were near the back of the shop.
When they walked to the end of the aisle,
they saw a big archway with the words
"Puppy Grooming Parlour" written in
curly red letters. Under the arch were
three uniformed puppy groomers, swarms
of puppies and a crowd of owners.
The groomers and the owners were all
shouting and waving their arms around.
And as for the puppies . . .

"Oh my goodness," said Kirsty, gasping.

There was a border collie whose silky
coat had been curled into ringlets and
decorated with at least a hundred red
ribbons. A husky's coat had been gelled

into spikes, and an unhappy-looking Pomeranian was modelling an 80s perm. There was a poodle whose curls had been straightened and an Afghan hound with a very wonky haircut.

"I'm so sorry," one of the groomers kept repeating. "I can't understand what's gone wrong today."

Rachel and Kirsty shared a worried glance. They knew exactly why the puppy grooming had been such a disaster. As well as volunteering at the shelter, they had been busy helping the Puppy Care Fairies. Naughty Jack Frost had stolen their puppies, as well as the enchanted collars that helped the fairies make their magic. The girls had helped to find Li the Labrador Fairy's puppy, Buddy, and Frenchie the Bulldog Fairy's puppy, Pepper, but two of the puppies were still missing.

"Until we find Wiggles and Cleo, everything to do with grooming and training will go wrong," said Rachel.

"Look at the state of my Japanese Akita," one woman wailed at the groomers. "He's gone blue!"

Read Seren the Sausage Dog Fairy to find out what adventures are in store for Kirsty and Rachel!

Read the brand-new series
from Daisy Meadows...

Ride. Dream. Believe.

Meet best friends Aisha and Emily
and journey to the secret world of
Enchanted Valley!

Calling all parents, carers and teachers!
The Rainbow Magic fairies are here to help
your child enter the magical world of reading.
Whatever reading stage they are at, there's
a Rainbow Magic book for everyone!
Here is Lydia the Reading Fairy's guide to
supporting your child's journey at all levels.

Starting Out

1 Our Rainbow Magic Beginner Readers are perfect for first-time readers who are just beginning to develop reading skills and confidence. Approved by teachers, they contain a full range of educational levelling, as well as lively full-colour illustrations.

Developing Readers

2 Rainbow Magic Early Readers contain longer stories and wider vocabulary for building stamina and growing confidence. These are adaptations of our most popular Rainbow Magic stories, specially developed for younger readers in conjunction with an Early Years reading consultant, with full-colour illustrations.

Going Solo

3 The Rainbow Magic chapter books – a mixture of series and one-off specials – contain accessible writing to encourage your child to venture into reading independently. These highly collectible and much-loved magical stories inspire a love of reading to last a lifetime.

www.orchardseriesbooks.co.uk

"Rainbow Magic got my daughter reading chapter books. Great sparkly covers, cute fairies and traditional stories full of magic that she found impossible to put down" - Mother of Edie (6 years)

"Florence LOVES the Rainbow Magic books. She really enjoys reading now" - Mother of Florence (6 years)

Read along the Reading Rainbow!

Well done – you have completed the book!

This book was worth 1 star.

See how far you have climbed on the Reading Rainbow opposite.
The more books you read, the more stars you can colour in
and the closer you will be to becoming a Royal Fairy!

Do you want to print your own Reading Rainbow?

1) Go to the Rainbow Magic website

2) Download and print out the poster

3) Colour in a star for every book you finish
and climb the Reading Rainbow

4) For every step up the rainbow,
you can download your very own certificate

There's all this and lots more at
orchardseriesbooks.co.uk

You'll find activities, stories, a special newsletter
AND you can search for the fairy with your name!